Hop-purr Hops Into Trouble

By Cindy West
Illustrated by Hallmark Properties

A GOLDEN BOOK · NEW YORK
Western Publishing Company, Inc., Racine, Wisconsin 53404

It was a lovely summer day. All the Purr-tenders were happy because they no longer lived in the Pick-A-Dilly Pet Shop. Instead they lived with their new owners, who knew their secret: They were all really cats pretending to be other animals.

Hop-purr was especially happy living with Amy Poole, because Amy had a big backyard to hop around in.

"Isn't summer the nicest time of year?" said Amy.

"It sure is!" agreed Hop-purr, hopping just like a bunny. "Summer's the perfect time to have adventures."

Just then, a real bunny hopped into Amy's garden! It wiggled its ears at Hop-purr and hopped over the fence.

"Here's my first adventure!" said Hop-purr, laughing. She waved good-bye to Amy and leapt after the bunny.

"Be careful!" called Amy, but Hop-purr was already too far away to hear her.

Soon Hop-purr caught up with the big white bunny. The bunny stopped in a huge garden filled with lettuce, tomatoes, and rows and rows of crunchy carrots.

"Yum! I'm crazy about carrots!" cried Hop-purr. "I can't wait to sink my teeth into them."

"Watch out for those tall bramble bushes," warned the bunny. "If you get too close, the brambles'll stick to your fur. By the way, what kind of bunny are you, anyway? You look a little different." But Hop-purr was so busy chewing, she didn't hear.

Soon the bunny finished lunch and hopped away.
"Hey," yelled Hop-purr! "Wait for me!" But when she
tried to follow the rabbit, Hop-purr got a big surprise—
she was all tangled up in the sticky bramble bush. Poor
Hop-purr couldn't move at all!

"Help!" she yelled. "Please, someone help me!"

"Well, well, well," growled a familiar voice. It was mean, grouchy Ed-grrr from the Pick-A-Dilly Pet Shop! He hated all the cats and loved seeing a Purr-tender in trouble.

"It looks like you're in a sticky situation," growled Ed-grrr. "But don't worry. I know what to do. As soon as I can sneak out again, I'll come here with a box and take you back to your cage in the pet shop. You just *love* cages, don't you, little pussy cat?" Ed-grrr grinned a ferocious grin and rushed away.

Hop-purr struggled to get away from the brambles, but the burrs hurt too much for her to move. "Amy! Amy!" cried Hop-purr. "Can't you hear me? If you don't come soon, Ed-grrr will take me back to the pet shop, and I'll never see you again!"

Amy was too far away to hear Hop-purr. But somebody else *did* hear her—Romp-purr, who was burying a bone at the end of the garden. Romp-purr dropped the bone and rushed over to Hop-purr.

"Help me!" wailed Hop-purr. "I'm caught in these brambles, and Ed-grrr is going to take me back to the pet shop."

"That's awful!" groaned Romp-purr. "I'll get help right away."

Romp-purr dashed out of the garden. "Hey! There's a *really* fast way to go for help." Romp-purr leapt like a puppy onto a laundry cart. "Ooh, these towels are so cuddly!" Romp-purr purred and purred with pleasure.

The woman pulling the cart smiled at Romp-purr and patted her head. "What a very sweet puppy you are. I've never heard a puppy purr before!"

As the woman turned a corner Romp-purr heard some familiar laughter and quacking. It was Flop-purr playing with his new owner, Kevin Evans.

"Hey, Romp-purr, watch this!" bragged Flop-purr. "Kevin taught me how to dive like a duck."

SPLASH! Flop-purr did a belly flop, and huge fountains of water poured all over Kevin.

Romp-purr grabbed a towel as she leapt off the cart.
"Thanks a lot, Romp-purr!" Kevin said. "I guess
Flop-purr needs a little more practice before he can dive
just like a duck. I'll change into my bathing suit and
show him how."

"No, no," protested Romp-purr. "Flop-purr has to come with *me* now. Hop-purr's in trouble, and we have to help her."

"I'll save her! I'll save her!" Flop-purr shouted as they dashed off together through a hole in the fence.

As the two Purr-tenders ran through the next yard, they noticed acorns falling down all around them. "Hey," complained Flop-purr. "That one just missed my head! Who's up there tossing acorns around?"

"It's *me*! Chirp-purr!" called a screechy voice. Chirp-purr was up in the tree, practicing to be a bird. She gave such a piercing whistle, Romp-purr moaned and covered her ears.

"Isn't Chirp-purr a glorious singer?" crooned Anita Rose, her new owner.

"Sure, sure," said Flop-purr. "She's really terrific. But right now I wish she'd stop singing and come with us. We've got to get Hop-purr out of trouble."

"Of course I'll help!" Chirp-purr screeched, and she leapt down out of the tree and joined them. Then all three Purr-tenders rushed toward the vegetable garden. They were in such a rush, they almost knocked down shy Scamp-purr.

"Where are you all going?" asked Scamp-purr.

"We've got to rescue Hop-purr," gasped Flop-purr. "I'm in charge of the rescue, of course. You're too young to help, so you better stay here."

"I am *not*," said Scamp-purr.

"I can't disappoint my friend Hop-purr," she added and followed the others down the road.

In a very short time the Purr-tenders reached the vegetable garden. Romp-purr was so happy to see Hop-purr again, she leapt on top of her and licked her face. "Uh-oh!" said Romp-purr! "Now *I'm* stuck in the brambles, too!"

"I'll get you both out," boasted Flop-purr. But try as
he might, he couldn't untangle them.

"Oh, my goodness! We're in terrible trouble!" groaned
Hop-purr. "Ed-grrr's coming back in a few minutes."

"I'd say *one* minute," shrieked Chirp-purr from a tree.
"He's heading this way with a box right now!"

The three Purr-tenders panicked and ran in circles. "Stop! Stop!" whispered Scamp-purr, as loud as she could. "Since I've become a mouse, I've been nibbling quite a lot. Mice are always nibbling at something. Well, I think that's what we should all do right now—*nibble* away at the vines. If we're very careful and chew *between* the brambles, I know we can untangle Hop-purr and Romp-purr."

The Purr-tenders formed a circle around Hop-purr and Romp-purr and nibbled, nibbled, nibbled.

"It's working!" Hop-purr shouted, waving her paws. "We're free! Now Ed-grrr can't take me back to the pet shop! But we can play a big trick on *him*." She whispered her plan into her friends' ears.

"Aha," snickered Ed-grrr as he ran into the garden. "My sweet little bunny's been waiting so patiently. You must be so eager to get back in your cage. Won't it be wonderful to live with me again?"

Just as Ed-grrr reached out to snatch Hop-purr, all her friends jumped out from under the weeds, flashing their paws and claws at him!

"Yeek!" screeched Ed-grrr, and he dashed away.
All the Purr-tenders laughed and waved to him as he
ran off.

"Oh, my," whispered Scamp-purr. "I've discovered some catnip!"

"Come on, gang. Let's jump in," shouted Flop-purr.

All the Purr-tenders jumped into the catnip patch and had a wonderful time eating and rolling around and around.

Then they ran home to plan another adventure together, purring all the way.